TIME-LIFE
Early Learning Program

Tales for a Stormy Day

ALEXANDRIA, VIRGINIA

My brother Nathaniel and I love to visit our Grandpa. He's the best storyteller in the world. He used to be a sea captain, but now he lives in a lighthouse. The downstairs is shaped like a ship, and we get to sleep in hammocks—just like real sailors!

Note to Parents

Tales for a Stormy Day is a collection of original stories and poems that present moral issues in a light and entertaining manner.

In "Beeblebean and Beebleboo," two groups discover they are the same at heart despite their outward differences. "How the Cuckoo Got Its Name" teaches the importance of telling the truth. In "The Day the Rooster Slept Late," a fancy-dancing cock learns the consequences of ignoring his responsibilities. "The Three Brothers" tells the tale of siblings who discover the value of cooperative effort. Finally, "When Lion Stole the Bluebird's Song" is a poem about a lion who must surrender his freedom when he takes something that is not his.

Each selection is meant to spark a dialogue between you and your child about social skills or standards of behavior. These conversations about the effects on others of right and wrong behavior can help your child begin to establish his or her own moral compass.

One morning last summer, we woke to a huge storm. The sea was wild and gray, and the waves crashed against the rocks. I was a little nervous, but then Grandpa knocked at the door.

"Ahoy, mates!" he said cheerfully. "A nor'easter's blowing!" (A nor'easter is what sailors call a big storm.) "It could last a while, but we'll stay snug and dry. I've brought you breakfast in bed! Eat up, and I'll tell you a story." And he did.

Beeblebean and Beebleboo

Long ago and far away,
A stone wall high and wide
Was built between two kingdoms
That were standing side by side.

BEEBLEBOO

On one side lived the Beeblebean,
The other, Beebleboo.
But why so high a wall (and
Who had built it) no one knew.

For many years, the wall did what
The wall was meant to do;
It kept the land of Beeblebean
Free of the Beebleboo.

And those who lived in Beebleboo
Knew not the Beeblebean—
Though both sides spoke unkindly
Of the ones they'd never seen.

"Take care! Beware the Beebleboo!"
Said those in Beeblebean.
"We hear they don't have any hair
And that their ears are green!"

"Take fright on sight of Beeblebean!"
Cried those in Beebleboo.
"We hear that hair grows on their toes
And that their ears are blue!"

Season turned to season,
And the years so swiftly flew.
And on both sides of the wall
The Beebles' fears just grew
                    AND GREW.

The wall stood wide. The wall stood tall,
And might still stand today,
Had not a little Beebleboo
Gone to the wall to play.

She bounced her ball against the wall.
She threw it in the air.
The ball then crossed the wall to land
In Beeblebean somewhere.

By chance, a little Beeblebean
With nothing much to do
Was sitting by the wall and saw
The ball from Beebleboo.

He picked it up and threw it back
To Beebleboo. And then,
She caught it and she tossed it back
To Beeblebean again.

The afternoon passed quickly;
Both were sad to see it end.
But they said they'd meet tomorrow,
And each would bring a friend.

Two Beebleboo, two Beeblebean
Played ball next afternoon.
And each one said they'd had such fun,
They'd get together soon.

The next day eight small Beebleboo
And eight small Beeblebean
Gathered by the wall to play
With those they'd never seen.

Soon all the little Beebleboo
and Beeblebean were there.
Balloons and balls and soaring kites
And laughter filled the air.

"What's going on?" the grownups cried.
"What makes you laugh and play
With those we fear and do not like?
How can you act this way?"

"They laugh a lot, and so do we,"
Said one small Beeblebean.
"So what if they do not have hair?
Or if their ears are green?"

"The Beeblebean seem just like us,"
Said one small Beebleboo.
"Who cares if hair grows on their toes,
Or if their ears are blue?"

"REMOVE THE WALL !" someone cried out,
Perhaps a Beebleboo.
Or it might have been a Beeblebean—
No one remembers who.

Together those with hairy toes
And those who had no hair
Removed the blocks and stones and rocks
Until no wall was there.

And on that day of balls and kites and
Laughter, one and all
Could see that all their differences were
Really very small.

Where once a wall stood wide and tall,
Bright flowers grow today.
And Beeblebean and Beebleboo
Are happier that way!

"**H**ave you ever been to Beeblebean or Beebleboo?" I asked Grandpa.

"No, Sarah," he replied. "But I've been to places like that, and I've met people like them."

"With green ears?" asked Nathaniel, his eyes wide. "And hairy toes?"

"Well...not exactly," Grandpa smiled.

Just then there was a huge crack and a crash outside.

"What was that?!" Nathaniel and I screamed.

"Nothing to worry about,"
Grandpa calmly answered. "Just a
falling branch. This old ship has
stood through storms
worse than this!

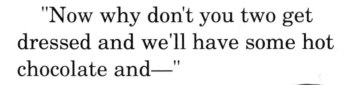

"Now why don't you two get
dressed and we'll have some hot
chocolate and—"

"And another story!" said Nathaniel.
"And another story," agreed Grandpa.

How the Cuckoo Got Its Name

Long ago when the mountains were just becoming mountains and the Great Ocean was only a small pond, Lion ruled over a peaceable kingdom of fabulous creatures.

Proud Ostrich flew faster than all the animals in the sky. Noble Tortoise was the swiftest animal on land. And shy Porcupine had the softest, sleekest fur.

But the most clever one among them, they all agreed, was Bird. So witty and amusing were Bird's stories that the breeze would stop blowing just to hear his tales.

One day, Bird was feeling restless. "It's too peaceful," he thought. "And too boring. What we need is some excitement." So Bird decided to play a trick on Ostrich.

"Ostrich," said the mischievous Bird,
"Lion told me that you will be able to fly even
faster and higher if you spread honey on your wings."
The vain and foolish Ostrich was delighted. He hurried
over to a beehive and helped himself to a dollop of honey, which he
smeared all over his magnificent wings.

"Hello, Ostrich," said Tortoise as she raced by. "What are you doing with all that honey?"

"Bird said it will make me fly faster," answered Ostrich.

"Hmm," thought Tortoise. "Perhaps honey will improve my speed, too." So she rubbed honey all over her four leathery feet.

Covered with all that sticky honey, Ostrich couldn't flap his wings. And Tortoise could hardly lift her feet, let alone jog or run.

"Perhaps we didn't put it on quite right," said Ostrich. "Let's go ask Lion what to do."

And so, with the poky Tortoise lagging behind, the earthbound Ostrich hurried off to find Lion.

As the two animals traveled through the forest, they dribbled big, gooey gobs of honey that fell on the pine needles beneath the trees. When Porcupine lay down for a nap, the honey stuck to her silky fur—and so did all the pine needles, leaving her soft coat a mass of prickly quills!

"Oh, dear. This isn't right," thought Porcupine upon waking. "I'd better ask Lion what to do." So she lumbered off after Tortoise and Ostrich.

The three honey-coated animals were a strange sight as they paraded across the plain. By the time they arrived at Lion's lair, they had attracted a huge crowd.

Hyena laughed and laughed. Cock crowed. Elephant trumpeted. Pig squealed. Monkey chattered from the top of a palm.

And Bird? Bird was simply delighted by the pandemonium he had created.

Suddenly Lion leaped out of his den.

"What's all this brouhaha?" he thundered. Then he noticed the strange trio assembled before him.

"Is that *you* under all those spines, Porcupine?" asked Lion gently, peering at the bristly beast.

"Yes," answered Porcupine. "I lay down to take a nap, and when I woke up I was covered from head to toe with sticky honey and prickly pine needles."

"Who spilled honey all over the forest?" demanded Lion.
Tortoise and Ostrich hung their heads. "We did," they
admitted. "Bird said it would make us faster."

"BIRD!" roared Lion ferociously. "How dare you disturb the
peace in our land? EXPLAIN YOURSELF!"

Bird, who had been thoroughly enjoying the spectacle, gulped.

"Explain yourself, Bird," the others squeaked and chattered,
hissed and squawked.

Cuckoo!
Cuckoo!

But when the frightened and embarrassed Bird tried to speak, he found that his voice was stuck in his throat.

"Cuckoo!" he croaked. Gone were the clever stories.

"Cuckoo! Cuckoo!" Gone forever were the amusing tales.

"Cuckoo! Cuckoo! Cuckoo!" That was all the lying Bird could say.

And from that day to this, Bird has been known as the Cuckoo.

And the others? Well, silly Ostrich never flew again, but he can outrun almost anyone on land. Tortoise remains sluggish, but she stops and smells the flowers she passes along the way. And Porcupine's prickly coat keeps her safe from enemies. As a matter of fact, in spite of the trouble that Bird caused, all the animals have lived happily ever after.

But not one of them listens to the Cuckoo anymore.

"William the Cuckoo Bird ever be able to talk and tell stories again, Grandpa?" asked Nathaniel.

"Perhaps," he replied thoughtfully. Then he got up and walked over to the window. "This gale's picking up, and ships won't be able to see the lighthouse," he said, peering out at the storm.

"I'd better sound the foghorn to warn them away from the rocks."

Grandpa climbed the long spiral staircase to the top of the lighthouse, and soon we heard the low boom of the foghorn.

"Now, who's for a game of Chinese checkers?" he asked as soon as he returned.

"I am!" said Nathaniel. "I want to be red!"

So we played Chinese checkers while the wind whistled around the lighthouse and the rain splattered against the steamed-up windowpanes.

"The winner gets to tell us a story," I said, after Grandpa had beaten us both.

"Alright," he said, "I will."

And he did.

The Day the Rooster Slept Late

Fred the red rooster
And Speckled-Hen Rose
Were dancing 'til midnight
On tip-tapping toes.

They tangoed, fandangoed
Beneath the bright moon.
They box-stepped and two-stepped,
While Fred hummed a tune.

"It's time you were sleeping,"
Said Rose with a yawn.
"For you must rise early
To wake up the dawn."

"Let's dance one more jig, Rose.
We're having such fun."
Then, whirling and twirling,
They danced until one!

Next morning—no morning!
The sun didn't show,
For Fred was too tired
To wake up and crow.

The sun slept on soundly;
The sun didn't know
That it should be rising—
For Fred didn't crow.

The hens softly slumbered.
The ducks and the sheep,
The farmer, his family,
And dog stayed asleep.

At noontime the farmer
Jumped out of his bed.
He looked at his clock—
Then went looking for Fred!

And all of the others,
Awakened by now—
The family, the dog,
The goose and the cow,

The chickens, the piglets,
The hens and the sheep,
The ducks and the donkey—
Found Fred fast asleep!

Cock-a-Doodle-Doo!!!

Fred was embarrassed!
He swore there and then
He never would let
This thing happen again.

Now Fred still goes dancing
With Speckled-Hen Rose,
But sets an alarm
So he wakes up and crows!

Just as Grandpa finished his story, the lights went out. Now it was *really* dark and scary.

"Oh, ho!" said Grandpa. "Now we'll have some fun!" He went to a shelf and pulled down an old oil lamp. He lit the wick, then adjusted the flame and brought the lamp over to the table.

The flickering flame made shadows dance on the wall. The room seemed even cozier than before.

"I've always liked these old lamps better than electric, anyway!" said Grandpa. "Now, how about some lunch?"

We followed Grandpa into the galley—that's what sailors call the kitchen—and made some macaroni and cheese. Afterward he wanted to take a nap, but we talked him into telling us another story.

The Three Brothers

Long ago and far away, in a place beyond the seventh sea, an Emperor and Empress had three wonderful sons.

The oldest son knew all the world's languages. The middle son was a marvelous acrobat. And the youngest son was a shy and quiet youth, whose only talent seemed to be that he could not be found when someone was looking for him. Still, like his brothers, he was a loving son, and the Empress and Emperor adored all three children.

Now, before you start thinking that the family had all it could desire, you should know that the three brothers did not get along with one another. In fact, they fussed and feuded and dickered and bickered about everything. And they might still be quarreling today had it not been for— ah, but I'm getting ahead of myself!

One day, the Emperor fell gravely ill. The seven imperial physicians tried many cures, but none could heal him.

"There is only one hope," the wisest doctor finally said. "The Emperor must drink a cup of tea made from the root of the jinjilly plant. But the plant grows only in the land of Jillypopo, and the journey there is long and dangerous."

"I'm not scared!" the youngest son said. "Let me fetch the jinjilly root!"

"No," cried the middle son, "you're too young! I will go and get it."

"I've known Father longer than either of you," protested the oldest son. "So *I* should be the one to go."

"Please!" said the Empress, anxious to put an end to the argument. "You must *all* go."

The brothers were not eager to travel together, but they knew that only the jinjilly root could save their father, so they set off on a bicycle built for three.

No sooner had the brothers started out, however, than they began to squabble. The argument became so heated that they didn't notice they were in the Wild Woods.

Suddenly a tiger blocked their path! "GRRR!" The brothers turned around and pedaled away furiously. But they could hear the tiger getting closer and closer.

"Help!" yelled the youngest brother. "Save me!"

Glancing behind them, the two older brothers were horrified to see that the tiger had seized the younger brother by the hem of his coat!

All of a sudden, the oldest brother growled. "GRRR!" The tiger looked amazed. Then the oldest brother growled again. "GRRRRR!" The tiger let go and ran into the forest.

"You saved my life!" cried the youngest brother. "How?"

"I have spent years studying all the world's languages," his brother explained. "Naturally, I learned Tiger. I simply told him that many tigers had tried to eat you before, and that they had all spit you out because you tasted so bitter."

By now the three brothers were hopelessly lost. Wild ginger vines hung from gnarled mango trees, blocking their view of the path ahead.

Without any warning, the bicycle plunged over the edge of a canyon! The younger brothers jumped off just in time, but the oldest fell with the bike.

"H-e-e-l-l-l-p!" he cried.

The two brothers peered over the edge and were relieved to find the oldest clinging to a branch. "Don't move!" yelled the middle brother. "I'll be right down!"

True to his word, the middle brother walked down the side of the canyon wall! He hoisted his astonished brother onto his back, then carried him up to safety.

"You saved my life!" said the oldest brother. "I thought only mountain goats could climb like that!"

"I have spent years training my body," said the middle brother. "Naturally, I learned to walk on canyon walls."

"Look!" cried the youngest. "There's Jillypopo!" Sure enough, across the canyon lay the land of Jillypopo. "And there's a bridge!"

The brothers rushed across the bridge. Jinjilly plants were growing everywhere, so they began to scoop them up.

"Halt!" boomed a voice. "Who dares to pick my jinjilly?"

A huge dragon loomed over the brothers.

"It's for our father," said the oldest. "He is sick and must have some jinjilly tea!"

"Well, maybe just a few plants," said the dragon, softening a bit. "But give me something in return."

"How about a trick?" asked the youngest. He spun around three times and disappeared into thin air!

The dragon was dazzled. "What a trick!" he said. "Take as much jinjilly as you like."

As the two older brothers gathered great armfuls of the herb, the youngest brother reappeared.

"How did you do that?" asked his amazed brothers.

"For years I have studied how to disappear," he answered. "Naturally, I learned to make myself invisible."

"Remarkable!" said the dragon. Then he offered them a ride home, and the three brothers climbed onto his back. The dragon flapped his wings and rose into the air.

As soon as they arrived home, the oldest brother set a pot to boil. The middle brother ground the jinjilly roots into a powder, and the youngest brother mixed the powder with the water to make a steaming-hot cup of jinjilly-root tea. The Emperor drank it and began to recover at once.

"My sons," said the Emperor. "You have braved many dangers and saved my life. How ever did you do it?"

"It wasn't easy," said the oldest.

"And," said the middle son, "we never could have done it —"

"—without each other!" said the youngest.

"**I** get it," I said knowingly. "Nathaniel and I should help each other do the lunch dishes, just like the three brothers, right?"

Grandpa laughed and said, "Why don't we all do them together? The work will go faster that way."

While we washed the dishes, we sang sea chanteys—that's what sailors call their songs. Then Grandpa let us rummage through his old sea chest.

"What's this, Grandpa?" asked Nathaniel, pulling a blue feather out of the trunk.

"Oh, that feather has quite a story," said Grandpa. "But you've had enough stories for now. I'm sure you don't want to hear another."

"Yes we do!" cried Nathaniel, jumping up and down. "We want to hear another story!"

"Please," I added.

"Alright, alright," laughed Grandpa. "I'll tell you the story."

And he did.

When Lion Stole the Bluebird's Song

Far away in Zing Zang Zing
The Lion heard thc Bluebird sing.
She sang of trees and clouds above
And other things that lions love.

And so, although he knew it wrong,
The Lion stole the Bluebird's song.
The Bluebird wept in grief and pain;
"Oh, woe is me!" she cried in vain.

When Bluebird tried to sing her song,
She couldn't sing—her voice was gone.
But Lion sang of stars he'd seen,
Of roaming free through grasses green.

Some hunters came along one day,
To take the Lion far away.
He tried to roar his fiercest roar,
The roar that kept him free before.

He tried to roar both loud and strong,
But now his voice was Bluebird's song.
The hunters weren't the least afraid
Of all the "Tweedle Dees" he made.

They heard him sing, they weren't upset:
They caught the Lion in a net.
They put him in a circus ring.
So sad—so far from Zing Zang Zing.

The circus went to Shim Boo Sham,
Then north to Flim and south to Flam.
While Lion sang to circus crowds,
No longer free, no longer proud.

He thought of Bluebird left alone,
Without a song to call her own.
And Lion yearned to right his wrong,
Apologize—give back the song.

The circus trekked to All-Ma-Taz,
Then west to Ploof and east to Fraz.
They traveled south, they traveled north.
They journeyed back, they journeyed forth.

At last they came to Zing Zang Zing,
Where Bluebird heard the Lion sing.
The Lion begged on bended knee,
"Take back your song. Forgive me, please!"

And Bluebird did that very thing:
Took back her song, began to sing!
Then Lion roared a fearsome roar—
The circus set him free once more!

Far away in Zing Zang Zing
You still can hear the Bluebird sing.
And Lion listens to her song,
But nowadays, he *roars* along.

And both of them are free.

"Now," said Grandpa as he finished his story. "Do you notice something missing?"

We both shook our heads.

"There's no more noise!" said Grandpa. "The storm is over!"

We jumped up and ran outside. Sure enough, the wind had died, the rain had stopped, and the late afternoon sun was breaking through the clouds. Pelicans and gulls skidded across the sky, calling to each other.

"Look!" said Nathaniel. "A rainbow!" Way out over the dark, swollen sea, there was a shimmering band of color.

"Red sky at night, sailor's delight," said Grandpa, studying the sky. "Tomorrow should be a lovely, sunny day!"

"Oh," said Nathaniel, sounding disappointed. "I was hoping it would rain again!"

TIME-LIFE for CHILDREN™

Publisher: Robert H. Smith
Associate Publisher/Managing Editor: Neil Kagan
Assistant Managing Editor: Patricia Daniels
Editorial Directors: Jean Burke Crawford, Allan Fallow,
  Karin Kinney, Sara Mark, Elizabeth Ward
Editorial Coordinator: Elizabeth Ward
Director of Marketing: Margaret Mooney
Product Managers: Cassandra Ford, Shelley L. Schimkus
Production Manager: Prudence G. Harris
Director of Finance: Lisa Peterson
Financial Analyst: Patricia Vanderslice
Administrative Assistant: Barbara A. Jones
Special Contributor: Jacqueline A. Ball

Produced by Joshua Morris Publishing, Inc.
Wilton, Connecticut 06897
Series Director: Michael J. Morris
Creative Director: William N. Derraugh
Editor: Lynn Offerman
Illustrators: Anthony Accardo (front cover, title page,
Grandpa's story pages); John O'Brien ("Beeblebean and
Beebleboo"); Yvette Banek ("How the Cuckoo Got Its
Name"); Andy Cook ("The Day the Rooster Slept Late");
Jerry Smath ("The Three Brothers"); John Wallner ("When
Lion Stole the Bluebird's Song")
Author: Muff Singer
Designers: Nora Voutas, Marty Heinritz
Design Consultant: Francis G. Morgan

First printing. Printed in Hong Kong.
Published simultaneously in Canada.

Time Life Inc. is a wholly owned subsidiary of THE TIME
INC. BOOK COMPANY.

TIME-LIFE is a trademark of Time Warner Inc. U.S.A.

Time Life Inc. offers a wide range of fine publications, including
home video products. For subscription information, call
1-800-621-7026, or write TIME-LIFE BOOKS, P.O. Box C-32068,
Richmond, Virginia 23261-2068.

CONSULTANTS

Dr. Lewis P. Lipsitt, an internationally recognized specialist on
childhood development, was the 1990 recipient of the Nicholas
Hobbs Award for science in the service of children. He serves
as science director for the American Psychological Association
and is a professor of psychology and medical science at Brown
University, where he is director of the Child Study Center.

Dr. Judith A. Schickedanz, an authority on the education of
preschool children, is an associate professor of early childhood
education at the Boston University School of Education, where
she also directs the Early Childhood Learning Laboratory. Her
published work includes *More Than the ABC's: Early Stages of
Reading and Writing Development* as well as several textbooks
and many scholarly papers.

Library of Congress Cataloging-in-Publication Data
Tales for a stormy day.
      p. cm. – (Time-Life early learning program)
      Summary: One stormy day, an old sea captain tells his grand-
children stories and poems to present lessons on how to live one's life.

      ISBN 0-8094-9307-1 (Trade). ISBN 0-8094-9308-X (Lib. Bdg.)

      1. Conduct of life—Literary collections. [1. Conduct of life–Literary
collections.] I. Time-Life for Children (Firm) II. Series.
PZ5.T225 1992   92-6170
398.27—dc20   CIP
                                                                          AC